Fast Forward

Fast Forward

JENNY PAUSACKER

Illustrated by Donna Rawlins

Lothrop, Lee & Shepard Books   New York

*The author wishes to acknowledge the
assistance of the Literature Board
of the Australia Council.*

First U.S. edition 1991 1 2 3 4 5 6 7 8 9 10

Library of Congress Cataloging in Publication Data
Pausacker, Jenny. Fast forward / Jenny Pausacker : illustrated by
Donna Rawlins.
   p.   cm. Summary: With his grandmother's new invention, the
Anti-Boredom Machine, twelve-year-old Kieran finds that he can speed
up time or travel back into the past, but this ability soon creates more
problems than it solves. ISBN 0-688-10195-X
[1. Time travel—Fiction. 2. Science fiction.] I. Rawlins, Donna,
ill. II. Title. PZ7.P2845Fas 1991 [Fic]—dc20 90-45762 CIP AC

For Beth

Contents

Play

Hi. My name's Kieran, and I'm twelve years old. But then again, maybe I'm twenty-four. I feel about a hundred. (I'll explain all of that in a minute.)

I have this really great family. They're all totally relaxed. For example, there we were at the start of this story—Mom and Dad leaning together on the couch, Flopsy and Mopsy squashed into the big chair, Cottontail sprawled on a pile of pillows.

We were watching our favorite movie on video—*The Empire Strikes Back*, we've seen it seven times. Well, actually we were still watching the previews before the movie. All totally relaxed.

Except for me. My fingers were going tap-tap-tap on the remote control for the video. My feet were going tap-tap-tap too. I was going crazy.

Finally I couldn't stand it any more. I pushed the FAST FORWARD button on the remote control. Cops and robbers started to run at top speed all over the TV screen, and a man cop and a woman cop bumped together in a kiss.

Then Flopsy and Mopsy moaned, "Stop it, Kieran."

Dad mumbled, "Yeah, take it easy."

Mom said lazily, "I like watching previews, even after I've seen the movie."

And Cottontail just grunted. She hardly ever says a word, not unless you practically twist her arm.

"All right, all right," I sighed. I took my finger off the FAST FORWARD button, and the cops and robbers slowed down to ordinary speed again. I sat there, watching the previews for the seventh time, and tap-tap-tapping.

Like I said, my family is totally relaxed. There's just one problem. I'm totally speedy.

I used to think I must be adopted—but look at Peter Rabbit. He went racing off

to get into trouble in Mr. McGregor's garden while his sisters, Flopsy, Mopsy, and Cottontail, stayed peacefully at home. So his family had two kinds of people in it as well—I mean, two kinds of rabbits.

(Yes, you guessed it. *My* sisters are called Morag, Catriona, and Lyla at school. But at home we still call them Flopsy, Mopsy, and Cottontail.)

And there's my grandmother too. She's little and sandy and wiry like me—the rest of them are all big and dark and round. And she talks fast and rushes round and gets impatient too. So at least there's one other person like me in the family.

Just as I was thinking about Gran, my mom said, "Bother. I forgot to take those cake trays around to Mom's place." After a while she added restfully, "Oh well, never mind."

But I was halfway to the kitchen door by then. "I can get to Gran's house and back in five minutes," I said loudly.

My family stirred and turned and looked at me. "But you'll miss the previews. You'll miss the first bit of the movie," they told me in worried voices.

I shrugged. "It's more fun if you have to guess."

Flopsy and Mopsy stared back—four big, round, puzzled eyes. "We like to watch everything," Mopsy said firmly. Then they quickly turned back to the TV, in case they'd missed something.

I tiptoed to the cupboard, eased out the cake trays, and ran.

I like running. A: You get there quicker. B: You can think at the same time. (I like doing two things at once.) As I ran, I thought that Gran probably wanted the cake trays for one of her inventions. Gran started off as a science teacher, but would you believe—in her day, women had to stop teaching if they got married. Newts to that stupid rule, though, because Gran became an inventor instead. She won a TV prize for Inventor of the Year when she invented the Smoke-Eater, which sucks up cigarette smoke. And her picture was in the *Women's Weekly* when she invented the Bounce-Bar, which protects you from bicycle crashes.

I came pounding up to Gran's door, but as I reached out to knock—oh-oh! I really must've been in a hurry to get out of the house—because I was still holding the remote control unit in my hand. Shoving it in my jacket pocket, I banged loudly on the door. Two seconds later Gran was there.

She was wearing her inventing clothes— bright yellow coveralls spotted with blotchy black oilstains. Before I could even say hi, she'd grabbed the trays and pushed me into the kitchen, where she started to throw dollops of cookie mix across the trays. "Say hello to your grandfather while I finish this," she ordered.

"Hi, Grandad," I said. Rats, I thought. No inventions today. Still, I liked cookies too.

Grandad looked up from his newspaper, blinked once or twice, smiled at me, and went on reading. (He and Cottontail can sit around together for hours, silent and happy.) Then there was a loud bang from behind us. The oven door slammed shut, and Gran was towing me out to the back shed, where she works.

"Got something to show you," she said over her shoulder.

6

Good, I thought. An invention *and* cookies.

The shed is full of long bare benches (because Gran tidies up as fast as she works) and huge heaps of wire and foam rubber and chunks of wood and plastic (because Gran never throws anything away). She climbed carefully onto a tall stool and reached up to the topmost shelf.

"Here it is." She landed beside me with a soft thump. "Look at this, Kieran."

I was looking at a shiny rectangle of gray plastic, covered with buttons that said FAST FORWARD, REWIND, PAUSE, PLAY, and STOP—just like the remote-control unit in my pocket.

"I hate to tell you this, Gran," I told her, "but someone's invented this already."

Gran shook her head till her hair fluffed out like a chrysanthemum. "No, they haven't. You don't use this on a video recorder. You use it on yourself."

"You mean . . . ?" I didn't know what she meant. "You play videos on yourself, instead of the TV?" Somehow it didn't strike me as one of Gran's brightest ideas.

"No, no, no. This has nothing to do with

videos," Gran smiled patiently. Then she scowled. "Oh, I can't be bothered explaining. Here, I'll show you." She folded my hand round the remote control and plonked my finger on the FAST FORWARD button. "Now, push."

I pushed, and the world rushed at me. Startled, I jerked my finger away. I looked up and saw—not the shed roof, but the elephant-gray branches of the fig tree in the backyard. Gran was holding onto the tree trunk and laughing like a kid.

"What happened?" I asked in a small voice.

"Well, we walked outside and—"

"I didn't walk, Gran. I almost flew. I must've looked all blurred or something, I was moving so fast."

Gran gave me a wicked look. "Dear, dear. I'll have to explain after all." She wrinkled up her forehead. "All right, Kieran, imagine you're watching a video movie. Then you push the FAST FORWARD button. Suddenly everyone in the movie seems to be scuttling round in a hurry. But the movie's the same, really, it just looks different to you. And when you use my new invention, life's the same, really, it just looks different to you." She smiled proudly at the little gray box.

I rubbed my head hard, as if I was trying to iron out a crease in my brain. Then my mind went into FAST FORWARD, all on its own.

"Wow!" I yelled. "So if you're waiting for the bus—or if you want to go to the pool, but your family isn't ready yet—or if some boring person starts talking about when you were a baby—"

"You can push FAST FORWARD and speed things up," Gran ended triumphantly. "That's why I call it the ABM, the Anti-Boredom Machine. It's my best invention so far." Her eyes glinted in the moonlight as she held out her hand for the ABM.

I hung on to it for a moment longer, stroking its plastic case. "Can I borrow it, just for tonight? Please, Gran?"

Gran looked flattered at first, but then she started to shuffle her feet. "I'm sorry, Kieran. You see, I discovered the ABM by accident—I was just trying to convert our remote control so that it could turn the sound up and down. I haven't had time to do proper tests yet. There could be all kinds of side effects."

I know about side effects. (Dad had side effects from some pills, and he got sicker instead of better.) So I had to admit that Gran had a point. She wasn't just saying no for the fun of it.

"Okay, you win," I said sadly and followed her back to the shed, still stroking the little flat gray plastic box.

I agreed with Gran . . . but all the same I couldn't stop myself from wanting to try out the ABM. You can try it later, I told myself sensibly, but that didn't comfort me. I wanted to try it now.

Suddenly my brain began to chatter away at top speed. If-one-button-works-then-the-other-buttons-might-too. If-one-button-works. If-one-button. Finally I couldn't stand it any more. I had to know. I held up the ABM and pushed the PAUSE button.

Gran stopped, one foot in midair. The wind stopped. All the sounds of the night stopped.

I shivered in the eerie silence. Then I pinched myself, hard. Good, I could still move. Before I had time to think, I pulled the remote control from my jacket and slid the ABM into the opposite pocket. Then I released the PAUSE button.

Gran's foot hit the ground. The garden noises rustled in. I handed the remote control to Gran, and she climbed up to hide it on the top shelf.

"I knew you'd like it, Kieran," she said with a grin. "I promise you'll be the first person to have one. Only . . . I may not get to work on it right away. To tell the truth, I love the ABM, but I'm a bit scared of it too. After all, if you made a mistake, you could go back to before you were born or, well—"

"After you were dead," I finished for her. Grown-ups are funny about death, even Gran. "I don't mind, truly. You don't need to hurry."

I was telling the truth, but I was lying at the same time. I didn't want Gran to hurry because I didn't want her to find out that she only had the remote control for our TV, not the ABM at all. I wasn't really stealing the ABM, though. I was going to sneak in at night and put it back.

Tomorrow. Or next week.

Gran gave me a huge bag of cookies, and I felt even meaner. I hurried to the door, waved good-bye, and started to run.

Right away I forgot all my worries because running on FAST FORWARD was fantastic. The trees zipped past. The road streamed under me like a river. The houses flicked by, too quick for me to count them. I felt as if I was on the fastest skateboard in the world. I felt as if I could win the Olympic games. And when I walked into the lounge room at home, I wasn't even puffed.

Dad looked up sleepily. "We stopped the video so you could watch the previews too."

"Oh. Thanks a lot," I said. Newts, I thought. I went to all that trouble to escape from the boring previews, and now I had to watch them anyway.

Tap-tap-tap went my fingers. Tap-tap-tap went my foot. Then finally I realized I was being a bit slow, just for once. I slipped my hand into my pocket and found the FAST FORWARD button.

The previews were over in a flash.

Pause

"Lights out, Kieran."

"Oh no, Dad," I moaned. "I just want to finish this page."

"No, you don't. You just want to go to sleep."

"Rats," I said. Hang on, I thought. I waved my hand like a magician and hit the PAUSE button.

Silence. No cars rumbling down the main street. No squeaks from Flopsy and Mopsy in the next room. I went to my bedroom door and peeked around. Dad was standing in the corridor, still as a statue. I thought about pulling a face at him, then decided against it.

Instead I punched up my pillows and settled down to read the next page. Then I read the next chapter, and the next. I was planning to read right through to the end of the book, when suddenly I remembered—you can't leave a video on PAUSE for too long, because the tape gets thin and snaps, or something. I wasn't a video, of course . . . but I didn't like the idea of getting thin and snapping. So I released the PAUSE button and turned off the light.

"That was quick," said Dad outside the door. He sounded surprised. "Good kid."

A grin spread slowly across my face until it nearly bumped into my ears. I lay back and watched the shadows dancing across the walls. From the beside table the ABM sang sweetly to me.

"Just wait till tomorrow, Kieran. We'll put a bomb under them. We'll make the world spin twice as fast."

I hate sleeping. It's such a waste of time. Once I tried to cut down to three hours a night, but after a few days my eyes prickled, my stomach felt hollow, and I kept bumping into things. So I gave up. I still reckon sleep is really boring, though.

I squeezed my eyes tight and started to count sheep. (Mom reckons this helps you go to sleep, when you don't feel tired.) But tonight the sheep kept turning around and talking to me.

"We like the ABM too, Kieran."

"Don't forget to buy a new remote control, Kieran. The old one's in your Gran's shed."

"Will you try REWIND tomorrow, Kieran?"

Finally I shooed the sheep away and did sums in my head instead. $7 \times 9 = 63 - 42 = 21 + 89 = 110 - 42 = 78$, no 68. . . . And next minute Cottontail was pulling my big toe to wake me up.

I stumbled into the kitchen and walked into the corner of the table. My eyes prickled and my stomach felt hollow, even after three slices of toast. I collected the ABM from my bedroom, but it didn't look so exciting in the morning light. It was just a flat gray plastic box. I shoved it into my pocket and staggered off to school.

Colin Cole was waiting at the bus stop. "Hi, Kieran," he called. "Did you see the new cop show on TV last night?"

"No, we watched a video," I mumbled, still half-asleep. Wrong answer. Now boring Colin would tell me the whole boring story, in boring detail.

And he did. "So then this big black car screams round the corner, and the cop jumps down—oh, I forgot to say he was on the roof of the house—"

I slid my hand into my pocket. "How long was this show, Col?"

"Two hours, it was a special. So the big black car slams—"

I slammed the FAST FORWARD button, and Colin's mouth started to waggle up and down, just like Donald Duck's. He didn't sound like Donald Duck, though. He didn't make a sound at all. There's no sound on FAST FORWARD.

It was fantastic.

But scary too. I mean, Colin wasn't on the other side of a door. He was staring me in the face. What if I looked weird, or

17

something? What if my eyes lit up, or I had wavy lines around me, like a magnetic field?

What if Colin could somehow guess that I was using the ABM?

I hung onto the FAST FORWARD button until the bus opened its doors in front of me. Then I jumped straight on, ahead of Colin. Mars and Tommy and Shana waved at me, and I pushed my way toward them. We started talking about the soccer team, and I forgot the ABM for a while.

Except that, as I got off the bus, Colin was waiting. I tried to hurry past, but he caught on to my sleeve.

"Are you all right, Kieran?" he asked anxiously. "I asked you a few times whether you wanted to hear about that cop show, and you didn't say no—but then you kept staring right through me with this blank look on your face." He fixed me with sad brown eyes, like the spaniel next-door pleading for a bone.

"Sorry, Col," I said, all cheery. "Didn't get much sleep last night. Well, see you later," and I strolled off with my brain buzzing.

I looked blank when I was on FAST FOR-

WARD, did I? Yeah, that'd be right. Usually, when someone's talking to you, you nod and smile a bit. But I couldn't hear Colin, of course, so I didn't know when to nod and smile.

Apart from looking blank, though, I obviously looked okay. No glowing eyes, no wavy lines. I was safe. I could use the ABM as much as I liked, and no one would ever know.

"Three cheers for the Anti-Boredom Machine," I announced out loud.

"Anti-Boredom Machine?" repeated Mars beside me. "That's a great idea—I could use one right now. It's yukko math, first period."

Actually, I like math. The numbers race across the page. "Subtract five from ten and you will get five": that's slow. "$10 - 5 = 5$": that's speedy. I always finish my math problems before the rest of the class. Then I stare out the window, or flick paper pellets at Tommy, or do some extra problems.

But not today. Today I just pushed FAST FORWARD and went zooming off to the next lesson. When I needed five more minutes to finish my map of Indonesia, I pushed the PAUSE button. When I got hungry, I FAST FORWARDed to lunchtime.

Hey, hey! I'll never be bored again.

After we'd eaten lunch, the four of us started kicking a soccer ball around, but Shana's shoelace kept coming undone, so she sat down to tie it up really tightly. Suddenly I had a terrific idea.

PAUSE.

All round the yard, kids froze. I saw a ball hanging in midair like a small rubber moon, a kid floating above her jump rope. I could've stared and stared . . . but I had a job to do.

Ducking around Tommy, I knelt and untied Shana's other shoelace. Then, slowly and carefully, I knotted both shoelaces together. (Luckily you don't need to keep your finger on the PAUSE button—it stays down till you release it.)

I dodged back to my place and released PAUSE. The ball fell from the sky, the jump rope turned, and Shana stood up.

Then she fell down again.

"What's the matter now?" yelled Mars.

Shana glared at him as she pulled herself up onto the seat. She looked down at her shoelaces, and her eyes goggled like a goldfish's.

"Shana tied her shoelaces together," I sang out. Tommy and Mars pushed past each other to have a look.

"It's true," gasped Tommy, and he started to laugh. We all laughed. We clutched our sides, we hung onto each other, we laughed till we were sore. Meanwhile, Shana just kept on staring at her feet and shaking her head.

"I did," she said at last. "I really did. I tied my shoelaces together."

Then she laughed harder than any of us. By the time we stopped we were too weak to kick the ball, so we went all around the yard, telling everyone how Shana had tied her shoelaces together.

It was my best trick ever. I only wished I could tell Shana and Tommy and Mars that it was me. But of course I couldn't tell anyone about the ABM, not even my best friends.

I didn't need to push FAST FORWARD once that afternoon. I just stared out the window and dreamed about the thousands of tricks that I was going to play.

I felt one hundred percent happy.

When you feel good, good things happen

to you. At soccer practice after school, I kicked this amazing goal. It should've been impossible.

I marked the ball on the boundary line in the left forward pocket, fifteen yards out. (And I'm a left footer.) When I lined it up, I couldn't see daylight between the posts. I sank a banana kick, and the ball sailed out parallel to the goal line. Then it slowly started to curl back toward the goalposts.

And through the goalposts.

The crowd went wild. (Well, Tommy and Mars and Shana went wild.) All the way home we kept talking about it.

"I think that's the best goal you'll ever kick in your entire life," Mars told me.

"Oh yeah?" I said. "Wait till you see the next one."

Tommy was thinking hard. Then on the bus he announced, "I've worked out a new invention for your Gran, Kieran. They do this operation, where they put a special little video camera behind your eyes, and it makes a movie of all your happiest times. So if you feel sad or anything, you can just watch the movie. Not bad, hey?"

"I bet you'd like to have a movie of that goal, Kieran," grinned Shana.

"Dead right," I said. Dead wrong, I thought as I jumped off the bus. Actually, I'd rather go back and kick the goal again in real life. So I pulled the ABM out of my pocket and pressed REWIND.

A giant hand zapped out of the sky, grabbed my collar and started hauling me backward. (At least, that's the way it felt.)

I was jumping backward onto the bus.

The bus was reversing back down the street.

I was running backward across the field.

It was weird. I mean, just think about walking backward. Normally, if you try it for more than a few steps, your knees start to wobble, you get this urge to look over your shoulder, and even then you soon bump into something. Not me, though. I was *running* backward, as easily as if I was running forward.

But of course I wasn't really running backward. I was really running forward backward, if you see what I mean. . . .

All of a sudden I started to feel incredibly dizzy. I jerked my finger away from the REWIND button. The giant hand let go of me, and I started to walk forward again.

Phew, I thought.

"I think that's the best goal you'll ever kick in your entire life," Mars told me.

I opened my mouth to answer him.

I was going to say, You'll never believe what just happened to me. I was going to say, Help! But my lips were already moving, and I was saying, "Oh yeah? Wait till you see the next one."

It made sense, of course. I was on RE-WIND, so I was in the past, so I couldn't change anything. I had to say the same things as before, I had to do the same things as before, even if I was feeling dizzy inside.

Oh yes, it made perfect sense—but just the same, I freaked. I hit REWIND as hard as I could, and I went running backward through the soccer game, getting dizzier and dizzier.

Then the ball hurtled toward me from between the goalposts. I wanted to duck, but I couldn't. Suddenly I realized that this was my goal—only backward. I shoved the ABM into my pocket and let go of the REWIND button.

I marked the ball on the boundary line. I sank a banana kick. The ball sailed through the goalposts, and I scored my goal once again.

I was jumping up and down, yelling, "I did it!" and waiting to feel the same rush of excitement, but instead—yes, that's right—I felt dizzy! I could see Mars and Shana racing toward me, beaming all over their faces. Any second now, they would start to say the things they said before, and I would have to say the things I said before, and I couldn't stand it.

So I pushed FAST FORWARD.

Some time later, I was sitting on the end of my bed with my head in my hands, wondering whether I was going to throw up. The first time I went on the Big Dipper I was sick as a dog, and REWIND was a trillion times worse.

To take my mind off it, I got out my secret notebook and wrote in big letters: "THINGS I HAVE FOUND OUT ABOUT THE ABM." I underlined the heading three times, drew stars around it, and then suddenly I was scribbling frantically.

1. FAST FORWARD is the greatest.

2. PAUSE is pretty good.
   a. You can play tricks on people.
   b. You can finish your maps and things.
3. I do not like REWIND.
   a. I get sick from going backward.
   b. It didn't feel the same, kicking my goal again. (Like seeing a scary movie twice—you can't get as scared once you know what happens in the end.)
   c. I went back and forth on the bus *three times,* which was very boring.
   d. I had to do all the same things.

I read back over what I'd written, nodding to myself. If you asked me, REWIND was a waste of time. Okay, you could repeat the good things, but you had to repeat all the boring bits as well. And you couldn't change the past. That was a huge letdown. I'd had a few smart ideas about REWIND, like, if I forgot my homework or broke something, then I could just push REWIND and get it right the second time around. But it looked as if I was stuck with my mistakes.

27

Who needed boring old REWIND, though? I still had PAUSE and fabulous FAST FOR- WARD. I had everything I needed, didn't I? There was just one thing missing.

I didn't have a new remote control for our TV.

I panicked. What if Cottontail told Grandad that we'd lost our remote con- trol, and Grandad told Gran, and Gran put two and two together and made trou- ble? I couldn't bear to lose the ABM, not yet.

I looked at my watch. It was no good— I could get to the mall in time, but I'd be late for dinner and the six o'clock news. But hang on, I could FAST FORWARD to the mall and be back in no time at all. No problem, I thought happily.

Actually, there *were* a few problems.

Problem number one: holding on to my bike's handlebars and the FAST FORWARD button at the same time. First I nearly dropped the ABM. Then I nearly steered in front of a semitrailer. After that I bought some tape at the store and stuck the ABM onto the handlebars.

Problem number two: My finger still kept slipping off the button, so I went FAST, slow, FAST, slow all the way to the mall. (It felt a bit strange, but I got used to it in the end.)

For some reason the TV store was closing already, but a nice woman let me in and found me a remote control just like our old one. Then came Problem number three: the price.

Who would've thought that a flat gray plastic box could cost so many dollars? Not me, I can tell you.

Well, I could forget about saving up for a skateboard. I didn't care, though. The ABM was more fun than a skateboard, any day of the week. I rode home—FAST, slow, FAST, slow—and bounced into the house.

Problem number four: Everyone was eating dinner and watching the six o'clock news.

"Where have you been, Kieran?" said Mom crossly.

"We've lost the remote control," said Flopsy and Mopsy sadly.

I shuffled my feet. "Sorry, I must've lost track of the time. And, um, I've got the remote control in my pocket."

I handed the remote control to Flopsy.

29

She pointed it at the TV—and for one horrible moment I thought I'd given her the ABM by mistake. But the channel changed, and we were watching the reruns.

With a sigh of relief I sat down to eat and worry about problem number four. What had gone wrong? I'd used FAST FORWARD, I shouldn't have been late. Maybe I'd stopped too often. Maybe the ABM didn't work on bikes.

Maybe I'd never know.

But an hour later, when I was doing my homework, the answer just popped into my head. In typical fashion, I'd known it all along. Actually, Gran had told me already.

"When you use FAST FORWARD, life's the same, really—it just looks different to you."

I got out my secret notebook and wrote in small letters at the bottom of the page, "P.S. FAST FORWARD doesn't make time *go* faster. It only makes time *feel* faster." Then I reached out and patted the ABM.

"Now I know all about you," I told it. "Now we can have fun."

Fast Forward

The next few weeks were magic. I was never bored, not for a second. The principal gave the school a big lecture, but don't ask me what it was about. I was on FAST FORWARD. Then my favorite teacher got sick and the substitute teacher was a real nong. Zip—FAST FORWARD again.

And I didn't have to wait around any more. I didn't have to wait for buses, or for the end of the last period on Friday. I didn't have to wait for the bathroom, or for Cottontail to decide between pizza and hamburgers for her birthday treat. Not me. I just pushed the FAST FORWARD button.

I kept well away from REWIND, but I had a lot of fun with PAUSE too. At first I just played a few simple tricks, like pressing

PAUSE and moving a chair or something. All my friends kept sitting down on the floor, or treading on their lunch, or hunting like mad for the ruler that was in their hand a minute ago, while I watched and grinned.

But then my ideas got bigger and better.

One day I thought, what if our classroom was haunted? Easy as winking, I pushed PAUSE and wrote "I am the ghost of poor Joe Blow" in red chalk on the blackboard. I added a few drips of blood, strolled back to my desk, released the PAUSE button, and listened to the screams.

Every day I thought of something spookier. Black candles appeared on the teacher's desk. (I found them in the cupboard under the stairs at home.) Joe Blow wrote more messages, saying that he was a kid who starved to death in detention twenty years ago. Then the spaniel next door dug up a pile of old bones—so some of Joe Blow's bones appeared in the middle of the classroom. Sophia Gianarelli and Dave Plover actually fainted.

I was still chuckling to myself that night when Mom wandered past, moving cushions and looking under newspapers.

I AM THE
GHOST
OF POOR
JOE BLOW

"What's the problem, Mom?" I asked.

"We never have any pens," she grumbled, kicking at the carpet.

"Yes, we do," said Dad, after a while.

Mom thought about it. "No, we don't."

"Oh," said Dad. He rubbed his chin for a bit. "Maybe you're right." (That's my parents' idea of a big argument. Like I said—totally relaxed.)

Anyhow, they'd given me a new idea. What if Mom's complaint came true and we really didn't have any pens?

Straightaway I set off on a trip around the house, gathering pens as I went. With the help of the trusty PAUSE button, I pinched Flopsy's ballpoint from the table in front of her, and then I remembered the stash of old pens in the kitchen drawer. Mom nearly beat me to it, but—zap! I pushed PAUSE and collected five more pens, while Mom stood there with her fingers frozen around the drawer handle.

Finally I hid about twenty pens under my mattress. Then I sat back to watch. Mom kept on hunting for a while, but at last she gave up and drove to the late-night store where she bought ten new pens.

I waited for half an hour, pushed PAUSE, and hid the new pens too.

By the end of the week Mom was wearing a ballpoint on a string around her neck. (You should've seen her face the day I nicked that one.) The pile of pens under my mattress was so big that it was making a lump in the bed, so I hid them in Dad's tool kit instead.

Next time Dad went out to work in the shed, I was waiting there at the window. He flung open the tool kit, whistling happily. Then his eyes bulged, and he went a kind of greenish color. He looked around guiltily, bundled the pens into an old newspaper, and tiptoed out.

A few seconds later the lid of the garbage can went clang.

I raced to the end of the backyard and laughed till I had tears in my eyes. Poor old Dad. Maybe he thought he'd hidden the pens himself, or maybe he just knew that he could never explain it to Mom. Either way, it was a great trick.

I wrote all my tricks down in my secret notebook—ten whole pages worth. I think I must've become the world's best trick player. Then somehow I started to lose interest. Everyone at home was grumpy all the time, and everyone at school was jumpy all the time, which got a bit boring.

Besides, when you play a trick on someone, you want to go, "Ha, ha, fooled you." And I couldn't. I couldn't tell anyone about the ABM.

So I didn't use PAUSE as much, after that. I kept thinking of new things to do with FAST FORWARD, though—like zooming at double speed along the school corridors, or running in the park with the world a green blur around me. I even rigged up a bit of wire to hold down the FAST FORWARD button while I was on my bike. Now, that was really speedy!

The Anti-Boredom Machine was the best thing since chocolate cookies. I couldn't remember how I'd gotten on without it. For example, there I was at the bus stop one Monday morning, with the bus hurtling toward me on FAST FORWARD. (No boring Colin Cole beside me, either—for some reason he always walked to the next stop these days.) I bounced up to Mars and Shana and Tommy, feeling great.

"Hi," they said in flat voices.

"Hi," I beamed. Boring. I thought.

I tap-tap-tapped on the back of the seat for a while. Shana and Tommy and Mars just went on looking flat, so I turned to stare out the window. The same old streets—until I pushed FAST FORWARD. Everything flashed past at the speed of light, and I started to feel great again.

First period was math with the boring substitute teacher, but that was fine, because I had my finger on the FAST FORWARD button—when in walked Ms. Zeybek, my favorite teacher.

"The bad news is, I'm back," she told us with a grin. "The good news is, I've got a lovely test, so you can show me how much you've learned while I was away."

My heart sank. I hadn't learned anything while she was away, of course. I was going to fail a test in my favorite subject from my favorite teacher.

Or was I? After all, I had a miracle wonder-working ABM in my pocket.

Actually, it was dead easy. I doodled in the margin for a while, then I pressed PAUSE and copied Mars's answers. (I changed a few things here and there, just to be safe.) I thought I was pretty smart, until the results came back.

Teachers are always saying, "Don't cheat, it doesn't really help you." They're right too—at least if you copy from Mars. Somehow I forgot that Mars hates math. He failed the test, and so did I.

But that was fine too. It was only one test, and I knew I could catch up. Except that Ms. Zeybek came in next day and said, "Well, now that you can solve equations in one step, we're going to learn to solve equations involving two steps." And I couldn't solve equations in one step, no way.

All right, I could've gone to the special class after school. But I'd always been good at math, I didn't want to sit around with dodos like Mars and Colin Cole. Besides, I had a better idea. I was going to travel back on REWIND and listen to all the boring substitute teacher's lessons. Okay, I couldn't change the past, so I still had to fail the test. But at least I'd understand equations in the future.

I really meant to do it too. But REWIND was so yukky, REWIND made me sick. I kept putting it off—and then I had even more days to REWIND. In the end I gave up and started to FAST FORWARD through Ms. Zeybek's classes as well. It was a pity, I used to like math a lot. Still, it was my only problem with the ABM.

Well, there was one other problem.

At lunchtime one day I raced over to Tommy and Mars and Shana. Instead of saying hi in flat voices, they said nothing at all.

"What's the matter with you?" I asked after a while.

"Nothing," Shana shot back. "What's the matter with *you*?"

"I feel great," I said, surprised.

"Then why do you keep walking past me in the corridor?" she asked.

"Why do you ignore me in math?" asked Mars.

"Why didn't you answer me on the bus, three times in a row?" asked Tommy.

Because I can't hear on FAST FORWARD, I thought. "Maybe I'm going deaf," I said.

"Deaf in your eyes?" asked Shana. "You didn't *see* me."

Well, how could I see her when I was zooming along at double speed? I started to get angry. "You should've told me before," I began. "You should—"

"I thought it was just me," said Shana,

and, "I thought it was just me," said Tommy, and, "I thought it was just me," said Mars.

"Then we got together," Tommy went on, "and we realized you were being mean to all of us. So you better stop it, or we won't be friends with you any more."

"I'm sorry," I said. Boring, I thought.

Mars studied me coldly, as if he was a lawyer and I was in the witness box. "Does that mean you're going to talk to us properly now?" he demanded.

I'd have to sit through boring lessons. I'd have to stop speeding down the corridors. In fact, they were practically asking me to give up the ABM altogether.

"No," I said.

I walked away to the trees at the end of the yard, pushed FAST FORWARD and waited till lunchtime was over.

Actually, I spent most of the next week on FAST FORWARD. I felt bad about Ms. Zeybek, and I felt bad about Mars and Shana and Tommy, so it was easier to skip ahead to a better time. Besides, life was much more exciting on FAST FORWARD. I could've gone on speeding forever . . . but I knew I had to stop.

So on Friday night I made a promise to myself. I wouldn't use the ABM once, not for the whole weekend.

Normal speed seemed pretty dull after a week of FAST FORWARD. I felt as if I was crawling around like a snail, and as for my family, sometimes I wondered whether they were moving at all. I sat through dinner, tap-tap-tapping on the table, while Cottontail chewed every mouthful twenty times. The minute she put her spoon down, up I jumped, but Mom waved her hand vaguely. (That meant she wanted me to sit down again.)

"Kieran," she said, "is something the matter?"

"No," I said. Even more boring, I thought. Everyone kept asking me the same questions.

"You see, we got a note from your school," Dad explained. "Your teachers seem to be a bit worried about you. They wondered if you were having problems at home." He shifted the salt and pepper around thoughtfully. "Are you, Kieran?"

"No," I said loudly. For some reason I wanted to burst into tears, so I pushed the PAUSE button until I felt better. "No, I

41

like you and Mom. Even Flopsy, Mopsy, and Cottontail aren't bad."

"What about school, then?" Mom asked gently. "What about Shana and Tommy and Mars?"

I felt like pushing FAST FORWARD, of course, but I stopped myself. I'd made a promise, hadn't I? Then I realized that I'd already broken my promise by using PAUSE.

Okay, FAST FORWARD it was.

I sat and watched my parents' mouths waggling for a while. When I let go of the button, Mom was murmuring, "If you can't say anything now, Kieran, that's fine. But I hope you'll talk to us soon."

I muttered something and raced up to my room, where I FAST FORWARDed till bedtime. Mom and Dad looked in from time to time, but I don't think they said anything. I couldn't hear them on FAST FORWARD, anyhow.

Next morning I woke to a bright winter's day, all gray and sparkly. Suddenly I knew everything was going to be all right. I bounded into the kitchen, and there was Gran, quietly drinking a mug of coffee.

"Well, Kieran," she said. She fished around in her shopping bag and brought out a small flat gray plastic box.

Suddenly I knew that everything was all wrong again.

I tell you, I'd never needed the ABM so badly. I desperately wanted to block out whatever Gran was going to say. But I didn't dare to put my hand in my pocket, even for a second, because Gran was the one person in the whole world who could guess that I was on FAST FORWARD.

So I gritted my teeth. "Wow, have you finished the ABM now, Gran?" I said with a great big smile.

Gran didn't smile back.

"Kieran, if I'm wrong about this, I'm very sorry," she said. "But—well, your mom told me you've been acting strangely. I thought about it for a bit, and in the end I tested the ABM again. It doesn't work. At least, it works on the TV, but it doesn't work on me." She stopped and took a deep breath. "Kieran, is this the ABM, or is it just an ordinary remote-control unit?"

I stared at the little box on the table, hating it. "Gosh, Gran, I don't know," I said. (I was trying to sound innocent. But I just sounded flat.)

"Well, I don't want to believe that you'd lie to me," said Gran. She dropped the little box into her shopping bag and headed for the door. "I'm working on a new invention now," she said over her shoulder. "Come and see it some time. Or just come and talk." And away she went.

I hate talking. Talking is really slow. First you have to find the right words—and then half the time the other person doesn't understand, so you have to start all over again and find the right words for them. I'd much rather do things than talk about them.

But just then I didn't know what to do. Everyone was mad at me, even Gran. Okay, they'd get over it in the end, but I still wished that I could skip the next few weeks.

Well, maybe I could.

I thought about our video recorder. If you want to FAST FORWARD for a long way, you push the STOP button first, and then you push FAST FORWARD. That way, you don't see any picture at all. The tape just speeds away inside the machine, until you press PLAY or the tape runs out.

Where would I go if I pressed the STOP button on the ABM? What if my tape ran out?

I was shaking—but then again, I was desperate. I sat there for a while with my

right thumb on STOP, my right forefinger on FAST FORWARD, and my left thumb on PLAY.

Then I pressed STOP and FAST FORWARD.

Speed speed speed, the fastest ever, speed speed, I'm speeding, speed speed, look at me. But no one could look at me, because I was nowhere, I was going nowhere, there was nothing but blackness and speed.

I knew I was speeding, because a sputter of yellow sparks ran through the darkness beside me. And I knew I was me, because a small spark of Kieran kept calling out, "Left thumb, left thumb, left thumb."

Finally, somewhere and somehow, my left thumb twitched against the PLAY button and I shot out into the world again.

For a while I just sat and blinked at all the colors. Then my eyes started to focus. A desk—so I must be at school, but the room seemed incredibly quiet. I looked around to find everyone scribbling busily. Rats, I thought, and checked my desk again. Sure enough, there lay the history exam paper.

I was supposed to write four essays, but so far I'd only written four lines. You can do better than that, Kieran, I thought. I picked up my pen and started to read through the questions, but pretty soon I realized that I was lucky even to have four sentences. I thought about copying from Shana. (She's good at history.) But I was really tired from all that sparky blackness, and I couldn't be bothered. I put my pen down again and waited till Mr. Kirby said, "Time's up. File out *quietly,* please."

Near the door, I bumped into Tommy. "How did you do?" I whispered with a friendly smile.

He sighed patiently. "Get lost," he whispered back. "I don't know you." He turned away and went on talking to Colin Cole.

I charged off down the corridor—and ran straight into Dad. That really scared me. I thought the ABM had mixed everything up. "What are you doing here?" I squeaked.

Dad gave me a worried look. "We're going to see the school counselor today. Don't you remember, Kieran?"

"Of course," I said quickly. "Just wait a minute."

I shut myself away in the toilets and thought fast. The exam paper. Tommy. The lines round Dad's eyes. It looked as though my life was still in a mess. Okay, I'd better FAST FORWARD to next year. With a smile of relief, I lined up my finger and thumbs and pressed the buttons.

I was used to the speeding blackness this time, so I could hear the little Kieran-voice more clearly, as it sang out, "Left thumb, left thumb." I pushed PLAY. And next minute I was sitting at another desk.

I was still in my old classroom though, which bothered me at first. What if I'd pressed REWIND by mistake? But the new teacher in front of the class was giving a welcome-to-first-term speech, so I relaxed and looked around.

I didn't know anyone. (Well, I recognized a few faces, but they were all younger kids. No one from my year, not even Colin Cole.) Newts, I thought, I'm in the wrong class. The bell went, and I was heading off to find my friends, when the new teacher stopped me.

"I'm really glad you're in my class, Kieran," he said. "There's nothing wrong with staying back a year," and I didn't hear the rest, because I walked straight out of the school.

I sat under the trees at the end of the yard, panicking like mad. This mess was getting bigger by the minute. As far as I could see, school was a dead loss by now. I didn't want to repeat seventh grade and make new friends. I'd rather just leave school and get a job. Then I could do what I liked, and no one could mess me around.

Yeah, that's a good idea, I thought. I could FAST FORWARD to school-leaving age, it was only four years. And after that I'd never have to be bored again.

Four years.

I jumped up. I was shaking. The ABM was in my hand, and I wanted to throw it down and stamp on it. But it wasn't the ABM's fault, not really. I'd pushed the buttons. I'd made a mess of the past six months, and I couldn't change the past, not even with the ABM.

I stood there, staring miserably at the small flat gray plastic box. No, I couldn't change the past, I couldn't change what I'd said and done. But . . . after all, for the last few months I hadn't really done anything much. I'd been on FAST FORWARD most of the time.

So maybe if I went back and lived through those months on ordinary speed, maybe somehow I could make things better.

Well, I couldn't make things worse, that was for sure. I straightened my shoulders, lined up my finger and thumbs, and, with a gulp, I pressed STOP and REWIND.

Rewind

Speed. Blackness.

REWIND. Sick.

Sick. REWIND.

Blackness. Speed.

"Left thumb, left thumb, left thumb, left thumb."

And somewhere in the whirl of darkness my left thumb pressed the PLAY button.

I plonked my hand down and looked at it for a while. Then I plonked down my next hand. The rest of me was stuck for a moment, until I shuffled my knees along. That felt good. I tried it again. Soon my hands and knees were plonking and shuffling at the same time. Even better.

I plonk-shuffled along until a huge piece of wood hit me on the head. That hurt. I opened my mouth wide, and out came a yell, right from the bottom of my lungs.

51

"Poor little lamb. Did he crawl into the table and hurt his head?"

Two big pink animals pounced on me and swung me into the air. I was flying. That felt good. But I didn't like the pink animals. I yelled again.

"Here, I'll hold him."

Two more pink animals, but these two smelt right. "Dad-dad-dad-dad-dad," I gurgled happily.

"Isn't that nice? He knows his father already."

"Well, actually he says dad-dad-dad to everyone. What are you going to say to Auntie Kath, Kieran?"

I burped. Then I curled up and sniffed at the good smell for a while. Then I was bored. That felt bad. I kicked, hard.

"He's a little fighter, isn't he?"

"Here, Kieran, do you want to crawl again?"

I plonk-shuffled around till I found an interesting thing. It was soft and gray and fluffy. It felt good in my hands. I pushed it at my face, to see if it felt good in my mouth too.

"No, Kieran. NO. You mustn't eat dust balls."

I knew about NO. NO was bad. So I

plonk-shuffled sadly away from the soft fluff. Then I saw another interesting thing. It was hard and gray and cold. It made me feel funny.

"Ub ub ub ub-ub," I said. (Well, that's what I said out loud. In my head, I said, STOP and FAST FORWARD.)

"What's he got hold of now?"

"I can't see. I'd better pick him up again."

The floor shook. The pink animals came swooping through the air towards me. I flung up my hands wildly, and they plonked down on the hard gray coldness.

STOP

FAST FORWARD.

Speed and blackness.

Blackness and speed.

 **Stop**

"Left thumb!" squawked the Kieran-voice.
Finally, I pushed PLAY.

I was running along the beach, with my cousin Sam just ahead of me. "I can catch you," I sang out, overtaking him. Then I looked over my shoulder. Sam had stopped to admire the waves. With a shout of "Slowcoach," I raced back and flicked him on the arm. He grabbed at me, but I ducked and dodged, and we chased each other in circles across the sand.

Inside I kept moaning, "Calm down, Kieran, please." But I couldn't change the past, so I had to run and run. Finally Sam yelled out, "I'm pooped," and flopped down on the beach. I danced around him for a while, then darted away to play chasey with the waves.

At last I had a chance to pull the ABM from my pocket. I hit the PAUSE button and sat down with a thump, shaking my head.

"Wow!" I said. "Wow, wow, wow! That REWIND is unreal. I went back to being a baby just then."

I said "Wow" a few more times, then I forced myself to think sensibly. Sam looked as if he was about seven, so I must be six years old by now. Six more years to go before I was back to normal. I'd better be more careful from here on out. I'd better try to FAST FORWARD one year at a time. Otherwise I might have to REWIND, and REWIND was always bad news for me.

I released PAUSE, and I was planning to push STOP and FAST FORWARD, but of course I immediately went zooming back to Sam. Hastily I shoved the ABM into my shorts pocket again, and then Sam and I raced each other back down the beach to the family picnic.

Mom waved to me and I dashed over to her. "Kieran, could you take your sisters for a walk?" she asked.

"Oh, no," I groaned. "They're so slow."

"Well, they're only little," Sam pointed out.

"I know, that's the problem. I wish they were big and brothers, like yours." I looked at Mom's big round stomach. "I just hope the next one's a boy," I said. (No such luck, I thought. The fact is, that's Cottontail in there.)

A ball went skidding across the sand. Automatically I stuck out my foot and stopped it.

"Chuck it over here, Kieran," called Sam's brothers. "Come and join in the game."

I looked round. Sam was walking away down the beach with Flopsy on one side of him and Mopsy on the other. So I snatched up the ball and ran toward the game.

I seemed to bat and run and catch and throw for hours. Normally I would've enjoyed it, but right then I was longing for the chance to push STOP and FAST FORWARD again. I was longing for a nice quiet time where I could rest for a bit. (But maybe I never had a nice quiet time. Maybe I was always racing around.)

In the end I dashed into the sandhills for a pee, and, before I could hurry back to the game, I got the ABM ready.

STOP

FAST FORWARD

"Left thumb," ordered the Kieran-voice from the rushing darkness, and straightaway I pressed PLAY.

I popped out in a classroom, with Mrs. McKinley smiling at us. (She was a very smily teacher.) Great, I thought, I'm in second grade. That means I'm seven years old, just like I planned.

I tried to remember whether second grade was nice and quiet. Mrs. McKinley was nice, I knew that. Perhaps I could stay here for a while. It'd be fun, in a way, listening to second grade lessons again.

"Well, class, who wants to tell us about their favorite book or film?"

My hand shot up. (Rats, I thought. Here I go again.)

"That was quick, Kieran," smiled Mrs. McKinley. "Are you going to talk about a book or a—"

"Film," I shouted, tearing down the aisle. I stood up straight, hands clasped behind my back, and gabbled rapidly. "My favorite film is called *The Vampire Bites Jack*, and I've seen it two times, and—"

57

And the whole class was roaring with laughter. Kids were clutching their stomachs and falling out of their desks and thumping each other on the back. Shana jumped onto a chair and shouted, "Shut up, you guys! Stop laughing at him."

"But—but it was so funny," gasped Tommy.

Shana frowned down at him. Then her mouth twitched, and she started to giggle too.

I was blushing inside and out. Hundreds of rats, I thought. Why did I have to live through this twice? Why did the ABM have to pick one of the worst moments of my entire life?

I stamped my foot. "Anyhow, *The Empire Strikes Back* is a terrific film, and Han Solo has this terrific old spaceship, and I'm not funny, so newts to you," I growled and marched back to my desk.

"Thank you, Kieran," said Mrs. McKinley kindly. "That was very good. It's not easy to keep on going after you've made a mistake."

I looked up at her. She wasn't smiling any more. She was sniggering behind her hand, instead. With a snarl, I punched

STOP and FAST FORWARD and hid away in the darkness.

"Left thumb, left thumb," the Kieran-voice reminded me, and reluctantly I pushed PLAY.

This time I was in the schoolyard with Mars and Shana. Mars was taller than the rest of us, so I knew we were all eight years old. (Mars grew really big when he was young. No one would ever fight him, except for Shana and Tommy and me. We knew he couldn't fight for peanuts, because he never got any practice.)

"Where's Tommy?" Shana was saying.

"Talking to that new kid," Mars told her.

Tommy came hurrying toward us, with Colin Cole in tow. "Hey," he called, "this kid knows some ace stories. Tell them the one about the magic skateboard, Col."

Colin Cole beamed. "I've got an even better one," he said.

Shana and Mars moved over to make room for him, and I scowled at them. "I thought we were supposed to be playing soccer," I complained.

"Come on, Kieran," said Shana. "We

always play soccer at lunchtime. I wouldn't mind hearing a story for a change."

"Me either," agreed Mars.

"Okay, you win. But I'd still rather play soccer," I said. No, I wouldn't, I thought. Colin Cole's stories were boring, but at least I'd get a chance to have a rest.

As soon as Colin started, my hand began to tap-tap-tap on my knee and my head began to turn this way and that. I wasn't exactly sitting still. All the same, I was quieter than usual. I got ready to drift away into my thoughts.

Actually, I didn't drift away at all. The story was about this kid who finds out that the principal of his school is trying to take over the world. No one will believe the kid, so he climbs up a drainpipe and videos the principal when he's plotting with his gang. In the end the principal goes to jail and the kid gets a gold medal.

It was a pretty exciting story, and Colin made it even more exciting. When the principal yelled at the kid, he put on a big booming voice. When the kid nearly fell off the drainpipe, he let out a yell. And when the gang was chasing the kid, he talked faster and faster. Tommy and Shana and Mars couldn't take their eyes off him, and I would've liked to watch him too. But I couldn't change the past, so I had to keep on looking round and tap-tap-tapping.

"Wow," Mars sighed happily at the end of the story. "Did you see that on TV, or is it a movie?"

"Neither," said Colin with a grin. "I made it up, just then."

"Wow," Mars was beginning again, when I pushed in front of him.

"That explains why I didn't like it," I said loudly. "I only like stories from TV."

"Oh, I know TV stories too," Colin told me eagerly. "I've got a really good memory for stories. I just wish I could remember math that well."

I gave him a friendly punch. "I bet you're good at soccer too," I said. "Any friend of ours'd have to be good at soccer," and I threw the ball at him.

He missed it.

Then he missed it three more times.

After that, he started to duck when he saw the ball coming. I shook my head sadly.

"Sorry, Col. Maybe we better finish the game on our own."

Colin looked relieved. "I'll just sit and watch," he agreed. "But listen, I could tell you a great soccer story later."

I could remember what I was going to do next, and I didn't like it at all. I wanted to push STOP and FAST FORWARD then and there, but I couldn't use the ABM in front of the others. So I had to dash around all over the yard, busily showing Colin Cole that he wasn't in our league. Then, when the siren blew, I slung my arm round Tommy's shoulder and dragged him away.

"Hey, what about the new kid?" he protested.

I shrugged. "He wouldn't have fitted in. He's slow as a wet week."

"He makes up stories pretty fast," said Shana.

I shrugged again. "Suit yourselves," I said and walked off.

Tommy and Shana and Mars followed, like I knew they would. They weren't going to pick Colin Cole over me. Then again, they didn't want to pick between us at all. They wanted soccer *and* stories, they wanted to be friends with me *and* Colin. Only I wouldn't let them.

It wasn't fair.

Usually, when you say, "It's not fair,"

you mean that someone else was horrible to you. But I was saying, "It's not fair," because I'd been horrible to Colin Cole. It was a creepy feeling, and I didn't like it one little bit.

So I pulled out the ABM and hit STOP and FAST FORWARD. Okay, I thought as I plunged into the blackness, I've been speedy and I've been embarrassed and I've been mean. Let's see if I can do better next time.

"Left thumb," commanded the Kieran-voice, and I pressed down.

The darkness cleared and I looked into a swirl of green. Behind me Dad was saying, "Are you *sure* you won't come for a walk, Lorna?" (I could tell from his voice that he was asking for the third time.)

"No, thanks," Mom said patiently. "Cottontail and I will enjoy the rest. Besides, it'll give you a chance to talk to your parents."

I glanced along the track and, sure enough, there were Nanna and Pops. Great, I thought, we're at the farm. I can relax and have a good time, for a change.

I went bounding off down the hill. "Don't run, Kieran," Nanna called after me.

"Yeah, yeah," I said. No way, I thought. (I hate people telling me to go slower.)

Next minute I was sliding down the track on the seat of my pants. When I scrambled up, Nanna was tut-tutting beside me. She started to belt the yellow mud off my jeans.

"That path gets really slippery after the rain," she said. Then she gave me a long slow wink. "See, Kieran? I don't tell you to watch out unless there's a good reason."

I grinned back at her. "I'll remember that next time."

Nanna paused to take a last whack at the mud. "No, you won't," she said.

We walked along together, watching the lambs. They bounced around the paddocks like springy toys, neat in their curly wool, their pink ears slanting back from their heads.

"I like lambs," I said.

"Just your kind of animal," Nanna agreed. "They never go direct from point A to point B, do they? They gallop and stop and jump in the air, then they gallop again."

I sighed. "It's hard to believe that they grow up to be sheep."

Nanna laughed and gave me a push. I

galloped off down the track, watching out for the thin brown trail of the river, gulping at the sharp country air, my skin tingling from the first spring sunshine. Inside, I kept trying to work out how old I was this time. Somehow, I couldn't quite place this holiday.

Still, it didn't matter, really. A bird was singing away overhead and I stopped under a big gum tree, leaning back to look for it. Then someone tweaked my ear, and I jumped like a lamb.

"So how's the running, Kieran?" asked Pops.

"Oh. Well. I'm doing all right at soccer."

Pops is—you guessed it—totally relaxed. All the same, he used to win prizes for running. He tried to teach me to run, but it didn't work. Mind you, I like running, I just wasn't too keen on the training. With soccer, you run and jump and catch and kick. With running, you just run.

Pops had been thinking. "It's one thing to be speedy," he told me. He thought a bit more, and added, "It's another thing to be a runner."

"You should know," I said quickly, and he tweaked my other ear. Then he started to tell me about the new tractor. (I was going to learn to drive the tractor when I was older.)

We left the track and set off down the hillside. It was really steep—Dad had to hang onto Flopsy and Mopsy in case they went too fast. This is my favorite bit of the whole farm. One minute you're walking along a grassy slope, and next minute the ground drops away and you're staring into this huge rocky gorge.

The river gets taken by surprise too. It's winding along quietly, minding its own business and—pow! It goes crashing down into a deep pool, kicking up spray in all directions. Then it picks itself up and winds on, an ordinary small river again.

We sat in a row and watched the waterfall in silence for a while, until Dad stretched and sighed.

"As I always say," he began, "you—"

"You can take the boy out of the country, but you can't take the country out of the boy," the rest of us chanted together.

(It's true. He always said the same thing, every time he looked at the waterfall.)

Dad blushed. "Well," he said loudly, "I still really love this farm."

"Me too," said Nanna. She put her hand over Pops' hand and they smiled at each other.

On the way back, Dad piggybacked Flopsy and I piggybacked Mopsy. It was getting dark by now, and the lambs were just white blobs in the shadows. As I caught sight of the farmhouse lights, Flopsy came running up, and Mopsy decided to show off. She bounced up and down on my back like a jockey, yelling, "Giddy-up, horsey."

First I scowled, then I had an idea. I dumped her on the track next to Flopsy, groaning pathetically.

"Boy, my feet are sore," I complained. "I was going to run ahead and surprise Mom, but I'm really tried."

I took a few limping steps and my sisters scampered away, giggling together. "Mom, Mom," they called out. "We're the first. We beat Kieran home."

I strolled after them, grinning to myself and looking round at the hills, all different colors of blue against the twilight sky. When I was little, I thought the hills really were blue. I wondered why we never drove down blue roads between blue trees on our way to the farm. Now I knew that the hills only looked blue, but I still liked them.

Behind me, Pops rumbled away, with murmurs from Dad and Nanna at regular intervals. I'm glad the ABM landed me on this day, I thought. Even now, when I'd finally remembered that this was the last time I ever saw Nanna and Pops. Two weeks later they were driving into town, and some boys were driving too fast.

And that was that.

The ABM was in my hand and I hit the PAUSE button, hard. Then I sat down in the grass and howled my eyes out. Somehow, I'd never felt all that sad at the time. It was just like a longer gap between the holidays. But now, seeing Nanna and Pops again, I realized I'd never see them again. (If you know what I mean.)

I got out my hanky and blew my nose. I've had enough of the past, I thought. I was sick of it, I wanted to get back to the present, as soon as possible. Just before I released the PAUSE button, I said quietly, "Good-bye, Nanna and Pops."

Then, without looking back, I pushed STOP and FAST FORWARD.

Change Channels

I've heard people say they wish they could be young again. Oh, wow! They'd soon change their minds, if they realized what hard work it was. I'd been a baby again, I'd been six and seven and eight again— and now I was worn out. I just wanted to swim along in the blackness forever.

But the Kieran-voice kept nagging at me. "Left thumb, left thumb," it squeaked.

Somewhere in among the blackness and the speed, I remembered that this was important. With a tremendous effort, I pressed down.

As the world fell into place around me, I felt a stab of panic. Where was I now? Had I gone too far this time?

Well, I was sitting at the kitchen table,

for starters, staring at an enormous birth-day cake. Fat chocolate letters spelled out KIERAN, and a circle of candles blazed brightly, but I was too scared to count them. What if there were twenty-one, for example?

I jumped up quickly, filled my lungs, and blew. Then I grabbed a knife and started to cut the cake.

"Kie-ran!" said Mopsy's soft voice. "You have to make a wish first."

"I already have," I snapped. I pushed on the knife again, and Cottontail's grubby hand closed around my wrist. I glared down at her.

Mom laughed. "You don't get your wish if the knife touches the plate," she reminded me.

"I won't ever get to eat any cake, at this rate," I grumbled back. All the same, I let go of the knife and Cottontail nodded, pleased. I wish that I'm twelve, I thought inside. I wish that I'm twelve. I sat there, tap-tap-tapping on the table, while Dad carefully cut six slices of cake, each exactly the same size.

"Well, Kieran," he began, watching the cake carefully as he loaded it onto plates.

"Well, you're twelve now." He looked thoughtfully into midair, counting to himself. "That's right, twelve. How does it feel?"

"Not bad," I said. Fantastic, I thought. (Except that I actually felt as if I was twenty-four. Well, how old *are* you when you turn twelve for the second time in your life?)

Oh well, at least I'd come out of FAST FORWARD at just the right time. In a week I would take the cake trays to Gran again, and then I would steal the ABM again, and then . . . but I didn't want to think about what would happen then.

I just wanted to spend a totally relaxed week with my totally relaxed family. I looked round at them lovingly. I had already finished my piece of cake, but they were still examining theirs from different angles, or peeling off the icing, or cutting their slices into tiny pieces.

For some reason, though, they weren't driving me crazy, the way they usually did. Actually, it was sort of restful.

To my surprise, I kept on enjoying the slow pace. But of course I couldn't change the past, so I also kept on behaving in my usual way. For example, one night Flopsy and Mopsy decided to build a tower with their dolls. Every time the tower fell down, they giggled happily and started again.

Finally I jumped to my feet. "Look!" I said impatiently. "If you put the biggest doll on the bottom, then they won't fall down."

While Flopsy and Mopsy watched with big round eyes, I stacked the dolls speedily together. As soon as I had finished, Flopsy reached out and prodded the bottom of the tower. It fell down. Giggling, Mopsy picked up a tiny teddy bear, and they started all over again.

I sighed loudly and stomped back to tap-tap-tap on the table. But inside me a small voice was asking, "What if Gran had shown the ABM to Mum and Dad, or Flopsy, Mopsy, and Cottontail? Would they've been interested in it, even for a moment?"

Probably not, I decided. They would've hated FAST FORWARD for sure. Then again, I couldn't see them getting into REWIND, either. Basically, none of them would ever need an Anti-Boredom Machine, because none of them was ever bored. I used to think that was stupid. (I mean, life *is* boring sometimes, isn't it?) But after all, my family wouldn't have ended up in the mess that I was in.

Not as stupid as I thought, maybe.

That night I took out the ABM again. I pushed the PAUSE button and found my secret notebook. Then, slowly and carefully, I started to write down the whole story of the ABM. Each night I wrote a bit more. I was hoping to find some way out of the mess—but instead I found out something even worse.

I couldn't change the past, right? So in a few days I was going to steal the ABM again, make a mess of my life again, push REWIND and become a baby again, grow up again, steal the ABM again, make a mess of my life again, push REWIND again—and so on, for ever and ever.

Flopsy, Mopsy, and Cottontail would grow up, but I never would. What would happen to me? Would I vanish? Would I die of old age before I turned thirteen? I didn't understand—but I didn't see how I could get out of it, either.

I didn't know what to do. So I just kept on writing in my secret notebook, going to school with Shana and Mars and Tommy, watching TV with my family. Hey,

I told myself, it could be worse. They're all terrific people. It wouldn't be too bad, seeing them again and again and again.

"No, it won't be too bad," I said. Just boring, I thought. Very boring.

On Saturday we were going to the zoo, but then the rain started to pelt down. Flopsy and Mopsy gazed out of the window with sad round eyes.

"I wanted to see the monkeys," said Flopsy.

"And the lions," said Mopsy.

"And the seals," said Flopsy.

"And the elephants," said Mopsy.

"And *all* the animals," I finished impatiently.

"Never mind," Mom told us kindly. She considered for a moment. "We'll rent a video tomorrow. Which one will we get?"

"*The Empire Strikes Back*," I yawned. "We always do."

"Now, Kieran," murmured Dad. "We have to think about it first."

Then he suggested *A Night at the Opera,* and Flopsy wondered about *Alice in Wonderland,* and Mopsy thought of *The Dark Crystal,* and Mom tossed in *That's Entertainment,* and Cottontail sucked her thumb and nodded to everything.

Finally we agreed on *The Empire Strikes Back.* (We always do.)

That night I got out my secret notebook, but I couldn't write a word. Why bother? After all, I could always finish the story next time I was twelve.

I wondered what I would do when I had filled up the whole notebook. I could never buy another one, of course. I could never do anything new. I was going to do the same things over and over, forever and ever. Me, Kieran, the kid who hated to be bored.

I was feeling really sorry for myself, when suddenly my brain gave a twitch. "Notebook," I said out loud. I sat there, frowning at a blank page, and then I yelled at the top of my voice, "That's it!"

This is what I realized:

A: I was twelve years and one week old, and I was writing in my secret notebook.

B: Last time I was twelve years and one week old, I most definitely hadn't written all of this. (Boy, that would've been a shock—to open my secret notebook and find the story of the next six months in front of me.)

C: So I *had* done something new, after all. I'd changed the past.

I was jiggling with excitement as more ideas came speeding into my mind. I hadn't had an ABM when I was a baby, had I? Or on the beach with Sam? Or at the farm with Nanna and Pops? I had changed the past by the simple fact of having the ABM in the past. And if I could change the past in one way, surely I could change the past in other ways?

But how?

All Sunday I kept asking myself that question. All Sunday, no answer. Willpower, I thought. I'll will myself to do something different. And two seconds later there I was, calling out to Dad, "Come here. I'm in trouble."

Wow, I thought. I've done it. I held my breath as Dad ambled down the path toward me.

"What's the problem, Kieran?"

I wanted to say, "It's the ABM." But I opened my mouth and said, "It's my bike chain. I took it off, and now I can't get it on again."

Newts, I thought. That wasn't willpower, that was what I said last time. I hadn't changed the past after all.

I watched sadly while Dad fixed the bike chain. Oh well, I'd just have to find another answer. I went on doing all the things I'd done before and thinking busily.

An hour later I remembered a show I'd seen on TV, about telepathy. (These two sisters could send each other messages through their minds—pretty impressive). I was alone in the living room with Mom at the time, so I concentrated hard and sent thought waves at her. *Help me, Mom, help me.*

Straightaway she put down her book. I was cheering inside as she looked up—to smile at Dad, who was strolling in with the video in his hand.

And then we were watching the previews—I was tap-tap-tapping—I was running to Gran's house—knocking on the door with the remote control unit in my hand—saying "Hi" to Grandad—looking at the ABM—stealing the ABM. Inside I kept screaming out, "Stop me, Gran. Help me, Gran. You'll know what to do." But I could only say what I'd said before.

Gran gave me a huge bag of cookies and I hurried to the door and waved good-bye. In a second I would start to run, I would start to do everything I'd done before.

NO!

Without thinking, I thrust my hand into

my pocket and hit the PAUSE button. I just needed a bit more time, I'd get the answer in a minute. . . . Then I realized I was holding the answer in my hand.

Up until now, whenever I pressed PAUSE, I'd always gone back to the place where I started from, before I released the PAUSE button. But this time I took a deep breath and deliberately walked through the open door, past Gran, and into the kitchen. I released PAUSE and leaned against a chair, fingers crossed. Gran bustled into the kitchen and hoisted a pot of soup from the stove, then she turned and dropped the pot heavily on the table.

"Kieran! How did you get in again?"

"He appeared," Grandad murmured from behind his newspaper. "One minute he wasn't here, and the next minute he was." He thought about it. "Very strange."

A frown dug into Gran's forehead. "Kieran," she said severely, "I think we'd better have a chat."

Grandad rose to his feet, folding his paper carefully. As he wandered past to the next room, he gave me a slow wink. I smiled back shakily, and then I faced Gran.

"Yes, I stole the ABM," I said in a rush. "And I went too far on FAST FORWARD, and then I tried to REWIND and I turned into a baby, and now I'm here again, but I'm scared I'll go round in circles forever."

Silence. I could almost hear Gran thinking. "Hmm," she said at last. "Well, you obviously didn't talk to me like this the first time around. So you've managed to change something. That's interesting—I thought you couldn't change the past."

"Me too," I said eagerly, and then I was telling her the whole story. Gran nodded and hummed and asked a lot of questions. Finally she held out her hand. I looked at it doubtfully.

"I'm congratulating you," she snapped impatiently. "You did well—in the end." We shook hands solemnly across the pot of soup, and then Gran pulled away, snapping her fingers.

"I've just thought of something else! You brought your ABM here with you, didn't you? But you also stole an ABM from the workshop for the second time." Her eyes glittered. "Tell me, do you have one ABM in your pocket now . . . or two?"

My mouth dropped open. After a moment's pause I cautiously patted my pockets. "I had my ABM in my left pocket, then I put your ABM in my right pocket. Or did

I put them both in the same pocket? Anyhow, I've only got one ABM now," I ended with a shiver.

"Only one," Gran repeated happily. "I wonder whether they melted together, or whether one ABM just disappeared—and if so, which one." I could hear her thinking again. She was getting excited about the ABM, just like I had.

I pulled the ABM out of my pocket and studied it. A small flat gray plastic box, that's all it was. *All,* I thought bitterly. A lot of trouble had come out of that little box.

"Gran," I said slowly, "you were right in the first place, when you wanted to hide the ABM away for a while. And I was wrong to take it." I held it out across the table toward her.

Gran hesitated and reached out. Her fingers were closing on the ABM, and mine were letting go. And next minute the ABM dropped with a splash into the pot of soup between us. As we watched, five bubbles rose to the surface and popped, one by one.

"Rats," I said. Good, I thought.

"Good," said Gran at the same moment, and we started to laugh. Gran grabbed a

ladle and tried to fish the ABM out of the soup, but her hand shook from laughing, and the ABM kept sliding back in. Finally she tipped the soup down the sink.

"Couldn't have eaten it anyway," she told me as she dried the ABM with a tea towel. Then she went bustling out to the shed, and I watched, wide-eyed, while she nailed the ABM to the wall.

"Why did you do that?" I asked.

Gran put her arm round my shoulder. "The ABM had its problems, but I liked it," she said sadly. "If we hadn't drowned it, I might've shown it to someone someday. And they might've made more ABMs. And in the end everyone in the world might've been racing round on FAST FORWARD, making a terrible mess. So now the ABM will always remind me to think about my inventions." She gave me a brisk hug. "Now, Kieran, what about you?"

I rubbed my cheek against her yellow coverall. "I think I'll be all right. I mean, the ABM's drowned, and I've changed the past, so I should be safe. Shouldn't I?" I added in a small voice.

"I hope so." Gran ruffled my hair. "Come on, let's get those cookies."

As I left the shed, I turned back for a last look at the ABM. Then I went racing into the kitchen.

"Hey," I yelled, "I never thought of changing channels. Did you? What's on the other channels?"

"Other worlds, maybe." Gran was busy already, of course, but the can opener dropped from her hand as she stared dreamily into the distance. "I wanted to try it, believe me, but I was worried that I might never get back." She shook herself briskly and smiled over at Grandad, still quietly reading his paper in the next room. "And I like this world far too much for that."

"I would've tried the other worlds," I boasted. Then I added quickly, "But not now. I've changed, Gran. I'm not going to rush around any more. I'm going to be totally relaxed, just like the rest of the family."

Gran whisked a tea towel around the soup pot. "Huh," she snorted, tipping two cans of soup into the pot. "Nothing wrong with a bit of speed, if you enjoy it." She slammed the pot on the stove and thrust a huge bag of cookies into my arms. Then she paused for a moment. "Kieran . . . would you like me to walk home with you?"

I straightened my shoulders. "No, I'll be fine, Gran." I hugged her again. Then I hurried to the door, waved good-bye, and started to run.

I like running. A: You get there quicker. B: You can think at the same time. But this time there was one small problem—I couldn't stop running. I want to get home, that's all, I thought. I could stop if I really wanted to, I thought.

Maybe I couldn't, though. Maybe I had to repeat everything after all, even without the ABM.

When I walked into the lounge room at home, I was shivering inside. Dad looked up sleepily. "We stopped the video so you could watch the previews too," he said.

"Oh. Thanks a lot," I said. Rats, I thought. So I added, "But don't bother, next time. I *wanted* to skip the previews, that's why I went to Gran's."

I sat down suddenly, knees weak with relief. I hadn't said that last time, I was positive. My ears were ringing so loudly that I could hardly hear Flopsy's and Mopsy's surprised squeaks. But I heard Cottontail's sniff.

"Of course he wanted to miss the previews," she said scornfully. "Kieran's speedy, like me. Only he rushes around, and I sit still and think fast."

She turned her back on us and went on looking at the TV. We all stared at her in silence, too stunned to say a word. Finally Mom drifted across and pushed the PLAY button on the video recorder. The previews started to roll.

I gazed round happily at my family. There we sat, all totally relaxed. Then I took a second look at Cottontail. She'd always seemed like the slowest person in the family—but maybe she was actually the fastest, in her own way. I could learn a lot from Cottontail, I thought. Well, I could learn a lot from my whole family. The ABM had shown me that.

The ABM had taught me other things, as well. In the future, I would always try to be totally relaxed. I would never be bored again. My family would never drive me crazy again.

Not even when they wanted to watch the previews for the seventh time.

Just then, out of the corner of my eye, I spotted something moving on the arm of the chair. I glanced down and goggled with surprise.

My fingers! They were tap-tap-tapping. . . .

And at exactly the same moment I remembered a terrible thing. I'd left our remote control unit at Gran's house. So, even if I wanted to, I couldn't FAST FORWARD the previews.

Though of course I didn't want to. Of course.

Tap-tap-tap.

Tap-tap-tap.

Tap-tap-tap.